Other books by Jeremy Strong

THE KARATE PRINCESS
THE KARATE PRINCESS AND THE CUT-THROAT ROBBERS
THE KARATE PRINCESS TO THE RESCUE

THE AIR-RAID SHELTER
FATBAG: THE DEMON VACUUM CLEANER
THE INDOOR PIRATES
LIGHTNING LUCY
MY DAD'S GOT AN ALLIGATOR!
THERE'S A PHARAOH IN OUR BATH
THERE'S A VIKING IN MY BED
VIKING IN TROUBLE

For younger readers

FANNY WITCH AND THE THUNDER LIZARD
FANNY WITCH AND THE WICKED WIZARD

Jeremy Strong

The Karate Princess and the Last Griffin

Illustrated by Simone Abel

PUFFIN BOOKS

PUFFIN BOOKS

Published by the Penguin Group
Penguin Books Ltd, 27 Wrights Lane, London W8 5TZ, England
Penguin Books USA Inc., 375 Hudson Street, New York, New York 10014, USA
Penguin Books Australia Ltd, Ringwood, Victoria, Australia
Penguin Books Canada Ltd, 10 Alcorn Avenue, Toronto, Ontario, Canada M4V 3B2
Penguin Books (NZ) Ltd, 182–190 Wairau Road, Auckland 10, New Zealand

Penguin Books Ltd, Registered Offices: Harmondsworth, Middlesex, England

First published by A & C Black (Publishers) Ltd 1995
Published in Puffin Books 1996
1 3 5 7 9 10 8 6 4 2

Made and printed in England by Clays Ltd, St Ives plc

1

A Wedding Surprise

'Ouch! That hurt!' King Stormbelly leapt into the air, looking for all the world as if he had just been stabbed with a long, sharp needle, which was in fact exactly what had happened.

Princess Belinda stood by her father's chair, holding the needle. 'It's your own fault,' she said. 'You moved.'

'Of course I moved!' roared the King, rubbing his arm vigorously. 'You stuck a pin in me! Now my arm hurts just as much as my head.'

The Queen gave her daughter a wan smile and turned to her husband. 'Perhaps your head would stop aching if you didn't shout so much, dear,' she pointed out.

'Shout!' bellowed the King. 'Who's shouting! I'll tell you why I have a headache. It's because of all these arrangements I've had to make for Belinda's wedding. Do this, do that, buy a present, order food, get a haircut . . .'

'You're bald Dad,' Belinda said calmly. 'You don't need haircuts any more. Now, sit still while I slip this needle in and you won't feel a thing.'

King Stormbelly backed away from his advancing daughter. 'Oh no,' he protested. 'Not again. I won't have any more of this achoo-punchyoo stuff.'

'It's not achoo-punchyoo,' said Belinda. 'It's called acupuncture and it really works – if you sit still. I learnt all about it when I visited Japan. They got it from the Chinese, who have been using it for thousands of years! You have to be very careful to make sure you don't do anything harmful. But don't worry, I've had months of special training. If you have a sore foot I can stick a needle in your ear and make the pain go away. If you have a headache the needle goes into your arm and it makes your headache go away. You won't feel a thing.' She took another couple of steps towards the King, who hastily hid behind a chair.

'Why do I have to have a daughter who goes round the world karate chopping people and sticking pins in them?' the King moaned. 'Why don't you behave like a proper princess for a change and try on your wedding dress? You're getting married this afternoon, and about time too. I've waited years for this moment. I thought it would never happen. After all, what kind of nutcase would want to marry a pin-sticker? Poor Hubert. I wonder if he realises what he is letting himself in for.'

The Karate Princess smiled a rather soppy, love-struck kind of smile. Of course Hubert knew what he was doing. They had been through all sorts of adventures together, and now they were getting married. Belinda had proposed to him when they were in Japan. Hubert had been very surprised, in fact he had fainted, but of course he said 'yes' as soon as he had recovered.

Since then time had rushed by. The arrangements had all gone quite smoothly, apart from Belinda and Hubert's great friend, Knackerleevee, wanting to be a bridesmaid like Belinda's fifteen older sisters. Knackerleevee was a Bogle, and Bogles are very big, very strong, very hairy and just a bit pongy. When Belinda tried to explain to him that Bogles did not normally wear dresses he had been most upset and had stuck the dress on top of his head like an enormous meringue.

Luckily Hubert had suggested that he was Best Man instead – or at least Best Bogle. Best Man! Knackerleevee was overcome. Fancy being called Best Man! He gave everyone an enormously proud grin. 'I'm going to be Bestest Man. Thank you, Your Royal-Nestingships!' And the Bogle went off to practise his wedding-speech.

By the time the afternoon had arrived Belinda was feeling a trifle nervous. She had been to the terrifying Marsh-At-The-End-Of-The-World. She had fought the Cut-Throat Robbers, faced up to steam-dragons and fought sumo-wrestlers, but she had never had so many butterflies in her stomach as she did now.

She stood alone in her bedroom gazing into the mirror. The reflection didn't look like her at all. She wasn't used to wearing dresses. It was all frothy lace and smooth satin, like sugar-icing. Belinda hated it. It wasn't her at all. She was only wearing it to please her parents. At least she had insisted on wearing her karate outfit underneath the flouncy dress. It helped her remember who she really was.

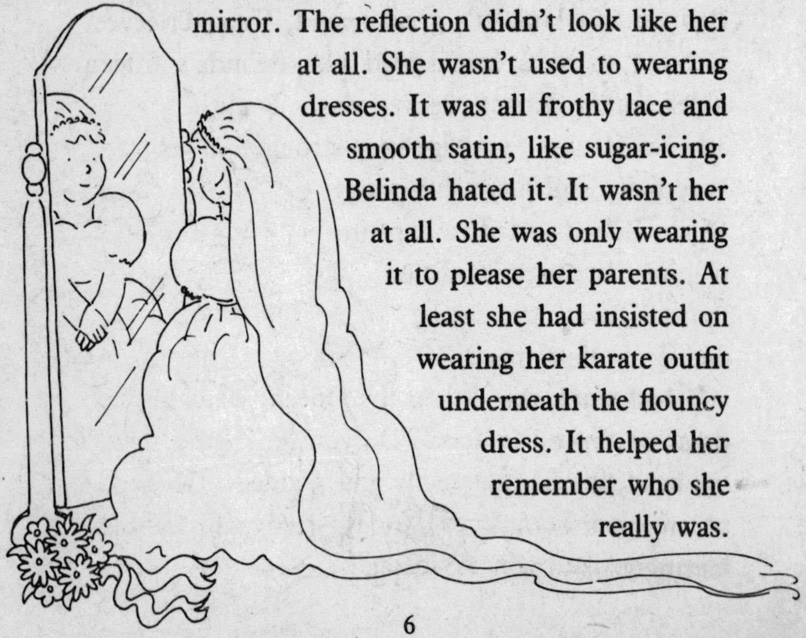

Belinda took a step forward to pick up her bouquet. But as she did so, she tripped over her flowing hem and fell flat on her face. Seething with rage she leapt to her feet and fixed her eyes on a huge oak chest of drawers in the corner of her room. The Karate Princess took a deep breath and sneaked up on the innocent chest. She turned her back for a moment, then suddenly whirled round, her right arm flashing out like a bolt of lightning.

'Haaa-akk!'

There was an almighty crack as Belinda's single blow split the chest of drawers in half. Bits of drawer spun across the room. Splinters whirled in the air and the Princess' clothes were flung lifeless to the floor.

'All right dear?' asked the Queen, watching her daughter from the door. 'Do you feel better now?' Belinda grinned sheepishly and nodded. 'Oh good. I'm so glad, because everyone is ready and waiting. Hubert looks really handsome.'

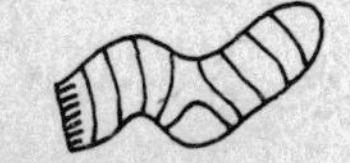

'That's because he *is* handsome,' Belinda replied.

'Yes, I know dear. I mean that he looks even more handsome than usual. Now, you take my arm and we'll go downstairs together.' The Queen glanced back at the smashed chest. 'I should think you might like a new chest of drawers as one of your wedding presents.' Belinda didn't say a word. As far as she was concerned, chests of drawers were exceedingly boring.

A great fanfare of trumpets filled the room as the Karate Princess appeared upon the royal staircase. The crowd cheered as Belinda made her way outside to where her father and Hubert, Knackerleevee, all her sisters and the priest were waiting. Hubert gave her an encouraging smile. King Stormbelly grinned like an ape and the excited Bogle stood on Belinda's dress with both feet without realising.

The priest looked at everyone encouragingly. 'Would the bride and groom step forward,' he asked. Belinda took a big step. There was a terrible tearing sound from round her waist and the bottom half of the frothing birthday-cake dress vanished. A gasp went up from the crowd.

'You great, hairy, clumsy, clot-headed SPIGGLY-THING!' spluttered King Stormbelly to Knackerleevee. 'Now look what you've done!'

For a few seconds everyone stared in horror, (and wondered what on earth a SPIGGLY-THING was). Then Belinda started to laugh. She threw off the top part of her dress and stood there in her karate clothes. 'Thanks, Knackerleevee,' she said. 'That was the best wedding present ever! I feel like the real me now.'

The Bogle grinned with delight, very relieved that he wasn't going to be executed on the spot. King Stormbelly went red and blue and purple and then back to red again. Before he could explode completely the Queen put a gentle hand on his shoulder and whispered in his ear. 'Ssssh. Don't say anything. Your youngest daughter is about to be married – at last!' The King calmed down at once and the priest went on.

'Hubert, – do you take Belinda to be your lawful wedded wife?'

'He means awful wedded wife,' hissed the King.

'Ssssh!' The Queen gave her husband a hard poke.

'I do,' announced Hubert, gazing at Belinda with adoring eyes. The priest turned to the Karate Princess.

'And do you, Belinda, take Hubert to be your lawful wedded husband?'

'I . . .'

But before the Karate Princess could finish, the air was filled with a great roaring noise and a gigantic shadow fell upon the wedding party. Everyone stared up in terror as a huge, jelly-like blob floated above their heads. A rope snaked down and two dark figures abseiled down it at high speed. Before Belinda had time to think, a sack was thrown over her head, her feet were jerked from the ground and she was hauled up towards the big blob.

King Stormbelly gave a strangled cry. 'Oh no you don't!' he yelled. 'You're not going to escape your wedding now! Come back at once!' He hurled himself after Belinda, and just managed to grab her disappearing feet. But it was no use. All he got for his trouble was one wedding slipper and then he fell backwards on to the ground with a dull thud.

The wedding guests watched in horror as Belinda was pulled up the jerking rope and stuffed into a rickety basket hanging below the hissing, heaving monster. Then the whole sinister contraption drifted higher and higher and further and further away until at last it could be seen no more.

'I don't believe it!' spluttered King Stormbelly, struggling back on to his fat legs.

'She's gone!' He turned to the priest and clutched desperately at the poor man.

'They were married weren't they? Please say they were married!'

The priest shook his head. 'I'm afraid Belinda hadn't actually said "yes".'

The King's face crumpled. In despair, the Queen gently patted his bald head and tried to murmur some soothing words in his ear, but even she was rather upset. This sort of behaviour wasn't expected at weddings. As for Hubert, all he could do was gaze speechlessly at the spot where his almost-wife had been snatched from his arms.

2

Grandees, Griffins and Gold

The Karate Princess squirmed and wriggled in the bottom of the basket. Quickly, she freed herself from the rather smelly sack and leapt to her feet, almost landing in a small but very hot fire burning in the centre of the basket. Belinda's first thought was to clamber out of the basket and make off at high speed. But a quick glance over the side showed that she was already several hundred feet above the ground. Belinda gulped and hastily pulled her leg back into the basket.

Her next idea was to knock out her captors with a few karate chops, but then she realised that firstly, she hadn't got a clue how to control the strange creature in which she now found herself, and secondly, one of her captors, an old lady with a face as wrinkled as a dried plum, looked rather familiar.

The old woman threw Belinda a quick glance. 'Hmmm – it IS you,' she muttered. 'Thank goodness for that.'

'Mulligatawny!' cried Belinda. 'What on earth is going on?'

'A very good question, and straight to the point as usual. Don't bother to say anything like, "Good afternoon and how nice it is to see you. How are you after all these years? Keeping well are you?". Excuse me, Princess, I must put some more wood on the fire.'

The old lady threw several logs on to the fire and flames leapt up inside the billowing canvas. Belinda was fascinated. 'What IS this?' she asked, and the old lady beamed with pride.

'This, my sweet Princess, is a hot-air balloon. Hot air rises. If you fill something with hot air, then it goes up in the air. This is a gigantic balloon filled with hot air. It floats in the sky.'

'It's very clever,' murmured Belinda, who was truly impressed, even though, being one of Mulligatawny's inventions, the whole thing looked as if it would fall out of the sky at any moment. It seemed to be made from the most threadbare piece of patchwork possible, and was all held together with bits of thin wood, knotted string and some kind of home-made glue that stuck to everything except the bits of balloon it was meant to.

'Hmmm,' muttered the inventor. 'It's only clever sometimes. If the fire gets too low or goes out then we fall out of the sky very quickly and splatter all over the rocks below – rather messy and not very nice at all – or clever. By the way, these are my two helpers, Scragg and Fink.'

The two muscled kidnappers grinned at Belinda. 'We're bodyguards,' declared Scragg. 'Guaranteed to look after you. Anyone comes along and tries to kidnap you, we jump on top of them and go biff-baff-boff!'

'Yeah – biff-baff-boff!' repeated Fink. 'See? I'm strong!' He wrapped one muscled arm round his friend's head and squeezed it hard.

'And – I'm – strong – too!' choked Scragg, reaching up a big fist and twisting Fink's nose until it almost came off his face.

'But you kidnapped *me*!' cried Belinda.

Mulligatawny looked faintly embarrassed, but not for long. 'Didn't have any choice, sorry. Didn't invite me to your wedding did you? Didn't even know you *were* getting married.'

'I wanted to ask you but I didn't know where you were.'

'Hmmm – maybe so. Anyway, that's not important now. We've got work to do. Ever heard of the Turnback Mountains?'

Belinda nodded. 'I've never seen them,' she said. 'But I've heard that they are so high, so deep in snow and so frozen that they are impossible to cross. Nobody knows what lies beyond.'

'I do,' said Mulligatawny, and a large smile spread across her ancient face. 'And that's where we are going. Now, listen carefully and I'll tell you a story about gold, power, great terror and one very important animal that nobody has actually seen.'

'Go on,' prompted the Princess.

'Remember the steam-dragon I invented? And that glider I made so that you could escape from the Tower With A Million Steps?' Belinda nodded. 'Hmmm, well, I've made other things too. I'm a good inventor – brilliant sometimes.'

'Yes, I know you're clever,' sighed Belinda. 'You said you'd tell me a story.'

'Hmmm. Well, one day this messenger appears at my door. Says his master wants me to make some machines for him – building a castle or something. Offers me vast amounts of money, so of course I agree and off we go. Come to the Turnback Mountains. I say to the messenger: "We can't cross these." He says to me: "You're right. We can't cross them. But we can go through them.".'

'Through them?' repeated Belinda.

Mulligatawny nodded and glanced upwards at the great mass of patched canvas heaving in the wind. She gave the fire a quick prod and flames leapt up inside the gaping mouth of the balloon. 'The messenger goes up to a huge rock and hits it with his sword handle five times, and it rolls back. Secret signal, see? Beyond the rock there's a tunnel, all lit with flaming torches, and lined with soldiers. We walk and we walk until finally I can see light at the end of the tunnel and we come out the other side of the mountains.'

The ancient inventor squinted up at the young Princess. 'We're in another country – another country which is surrounded by mountains, and in the middle there's this enormous half-built castle. The messenger makes straight for it and before I know what's happening, I'm standing in front of the ruler himself – the Grand Oompah of Pomposity.'

Belinda burst out laughing. 'The Grand Oompah of Pomposity!' she repeated. 'You must be joking!' The old lady scowled whilst Scragg and Fink stared at each other with horror-stricken eyes.

'Don't you ever laugh in front of the Oompah,' warned Mulligatawny. 'He'll have you boiled with his cabbage for dinner. I've seen him do it more than once. Anyway, this Grand Oompah wants me to build a digging machine. He's getting pink rock from underground to complete his castle and he wants me to make a machine to dig out the rock. So I do, and very good it is too.'

'Of course,' murmured Belinda with a faint smile. Mulligatawny didn't notice and continued with her story.

'Then I tell him I've finished and want to go home. He says I can't. Says I'm a prisoner there forever.'

'We were prisoners,' Fink suddenly blurted out. He jabbed a finger at Mulligatawny. 'She rescued us. We were slaves until she turned up.' He grinned again, showing a mouthful of black teeth. 'Now we're bodyguards,' he said proudly. 'Biff-boff-baff!'

'Not biff-boff-baff,' grumbled Scragg. 'Biff-baff-boff!'

'Knock your block off, Clod-head!' cried Fink.

'Tie your legs like shoe-laces, Pimple-brain!' threatened Scragg. Mulligatawny pushed them to one side. 'Always quarrelling. Just ignore them. They mean well.'

'Why did the Grand Oompah want to keep you prisoner?' asked Belinda.

'Doesn't want anyone to know he's there you see, not until he's ready.'

'Ready for what?' asked Belinda.

'I'll come to that in a moment. Don't rush me. Throw another log on the fire, we're sinking. I decide to escape, so I build this hot-air balloon to take me over the mountains. Then I realise I have to go back and you have to come with me. That's why we kidnapped you. Sorry about that. Hmmm. Couldn't stop the balloon you see. Dangerous enough having to come down low enough for the rope to reach you. Didn't dare land. Probably never take off again. Sorry about the wedding but we've got to go back and sort out the Oompah. I knew there was only one person who could help – the Karate Princess. So here you are.'

Belinda gazed out across the peaceful landscape below. 'Why do you need me? What's going on?' The old lady reached out and gripped Belinda's wrist tightly. 'Trouble. Very very big trouble. The Grand Oompah intends to use my digging machine to help him capture the Last Griffin.'

Belinda sighed deeply. The old lady's story was so full of things that she didn't understand. 'The Last Griffin? All right – tell me about the Last Griffin. I've never heard of such a thing.'

The sun was beginning to set and its red rays were glinting on a distant, sparkling line of mountain peaks – the Turnback Mountains.

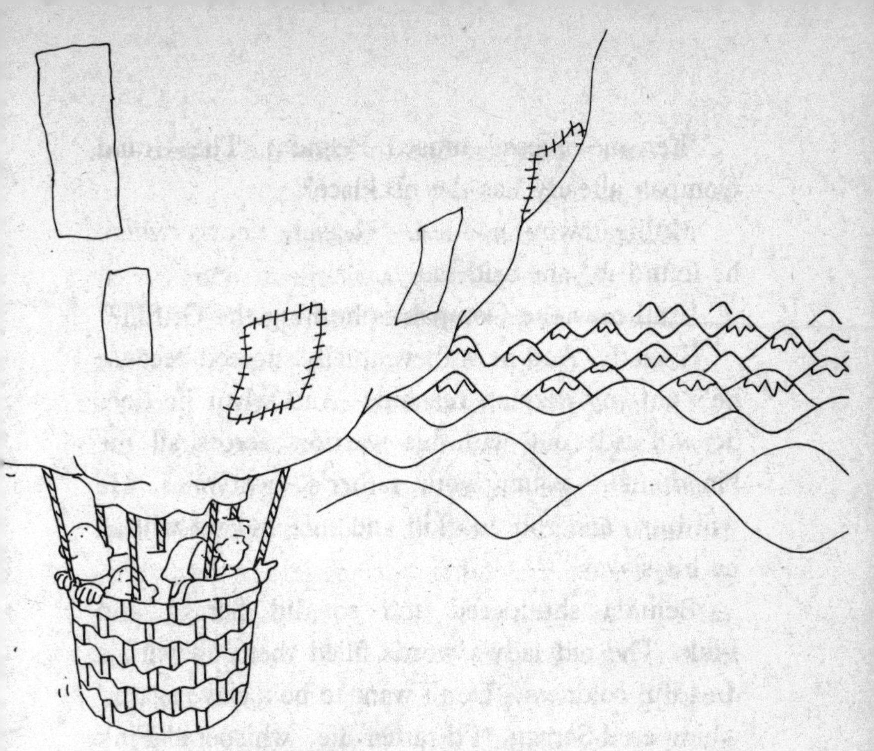

Mulligatawny pointed to them with a dirty, crooked finger. 'Somewhere beneath those mountains is the Last Griffin – a strange, secretive creature, and one of the world's last magical beasts. They say that one hasn't been seen for over a thousand years. It has a head like an eagle and the body of a lion, but with wings. It lives deep underground, where it guards the earth's hidden gold – a treasure so vast it would make you rich a million times over. People say that there is a magic necklace of gold and if you are able to place it round the Griffin's neck then not only are you rich but you also receive great power, because the Griffin must do anything you command once the necklace is in place.'

'Let me guess,' mused Belinda. 'The Grand Oompah already has the necklace?'

Mulligatawny nodded. 'Heaven knows where he found it,' she said sadly.

'And now the Oompah is hunting the Griffin?'

'Exactly. And he will eventually succeed because he's got my digging machine. And when he does he will ride out with his warriors across all the kingdoms – yours, your father's, everyones. He will burn and rob and kill and rule and we will all be his slaves.'

Belinda shuddered and so did Scragg and Fink. The old lady's words filled them all with a dreadful coldness. 'Don't want to be a slave again,' whimpered Scragg. 'I'd rather die,' whispered Fink with deathly sincerity.

The Karate Princess gazed grimly down at the glistening peaks that were passing just below in the gathering darkness. 'Then we must find the Last Griffin and fight the Grand Oompah until he's defeated,' said Belinda simply.

Mulligatawny's ancient face split into a satisfied smile. 'Ha-akkk!' she cackled.

'Ha-akkk!' grinned the Karate Princess.

'Biff-baff-boff,' murmured Scragg and Fink rather more timidly.

3

A Few Bumps and Burps

The night air was exceedingly cold. This was a good thing for the balloon as it meant it was easier to keep the whole contraption aloft. However, the four occupants in the basket spent the whole night shivering, despite the fire burning brightly in the grate. By the time the faint morning sunlight lightened the sky the balloon had passed over the highest peaks. Now it was descending, slowly but surely, and Mulligatawny was fretting over the fire.

'We're coming down too fast,' she muttered. 'We're going to crash and we haven't reached a safe place yet.'

Belinda peered over the edge at the sparkling snow. 'At least we shall have a soft landing,' she said cheerfully.

'Hmmm! It's not the landing I'm bothered about. It's THEM,' snapped the old lady.

'Them?'

'The Grand Oompah's Purple Police. They're everywhere.'

'Nasty,' murmured Fink.

'Horrible,' nodded Scragg. 'Make your eyes water.'

'Make your eyes pop right out!' said Fink rather more worryingly. Belinda tried to cheer everyone up, even though she was feeling a little nervous herself.

'Perhaps they won't see us,' she observed.

'They'd have to be blind then,' Mulligatawny said, and she pointed down at a large group of purple figures halfway down the mountain-side. 'We're being watched.'

It was true. The balloon had already been spotted, which was hardly surprising as it was enormous and coming down quite fast. 'Whatever anyone says to you, *don't* tell them why we're here,' shouted Mulligatawny. The four balloonists had just enough time to throw the fire overboard and crouch down inside the basket, before the whole caboodle crashed into the snowy foothills of the Turnback Mountains.

There was a stomach-churning sound of splintering wood. Air roared out from the punctured canvas and enormous folds of damp cloth flopped down over the basket, trapping the balloonists underneath. Belinda and the others fought their way out from beneath the smelly canvas, only to find themselves surrounded by forty exceedingly sinister-looking guards.

They were dressed from head to foot in deep purple. They had purple knee-length boots, purple trousers, purple jackets, huge purple cloaks and purple head-dresses that were wrapped round their faces so that only their glinting eyes could be seen.

'Don't move,' muttered Mulligatawny. 'Purple Police. Trained to kill anything that moves – even woodlice.'

Belinda had no intention of moving. These guards were heavily armed. They were waving long, bright swords with nasty pointy bits on the ends and they wore thick leather belts with at least five different types of dagger stuck in them. They even had extra daggers strapped to their boots. They were dressed to kill.

It was quite obvious that the Karate Princess and her companions had been well and truly captured. They were marched down the mountain, loaded into a cart and carried off into the heart of the Grand Oompah's land. Scragg and Fink were not very happy.

'What does it feel like to be a cabbage?' asked Fink.

'Haven't got a clue,' answered Belinda. 'Why?'

'Cabbages are boiled,' Scragg said ominously and after that there was a long silence, which was only broken when the cart rounded the bend of a hill and they saw a huge, towering pink castle directly in front of them.

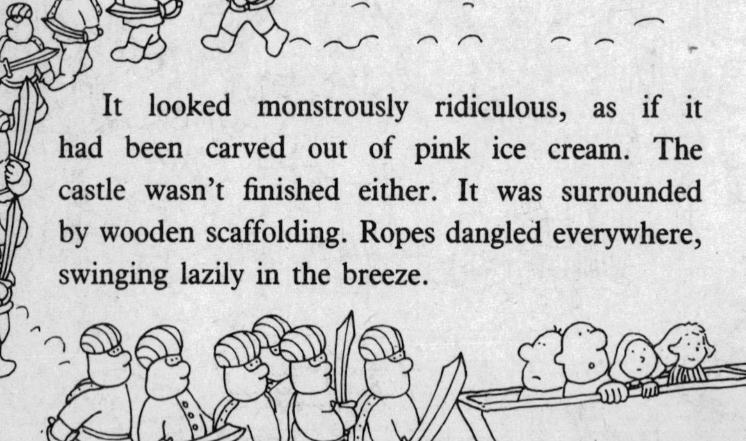

It looked monstrously ridiculous, as if it had been carved out of pink ice cream. The castle wasn't finished either. It was surrounded by wooden scaffolding. Ropes dangled everywhere, swinging lazily in the breeze.

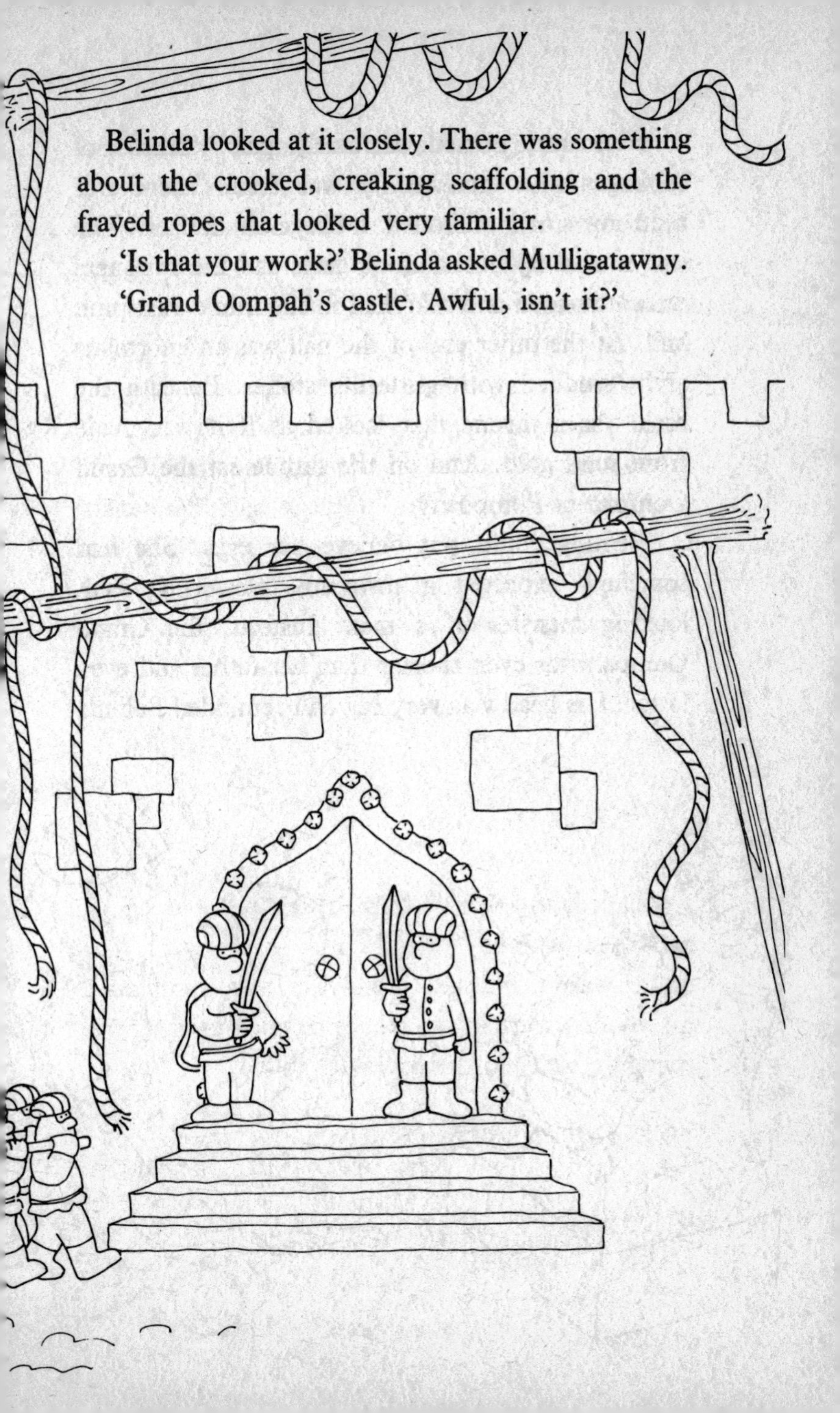

Belinda looked at it closely. There was something about the crooked, creaking scaffolding and the frayed ropes that looked very familiar.

'Is that your work?' Belinda asked Mulligatawny.

'Grand Oompah's castle. Awful, isn't it?'

Fink had turned extremely pale. 'Smells of cabbages,' he croaked. It was true. There was a strong smell of boiled cabbage in the air. The cart rattled up to the castle gates and the prisoners were unloaded and marched inside into a vast pink hall. At the other end of the hall was an enormous arch, studded with glittering stones. Beneath the arch was a throne that looked as if it was made from solid gold. And on the throne sat the Grand Oompah of Pomposity.

Belinda could not believe her eyes. She had somehow expected a towering, glowering, evil-looking monster of a man. Instead, the Grand Oompah was even shorter than her father and even fatter. His head was very big and reminded Belinda

of a large fish. He had big, round fish-eyes and a big, round mouth, bubbling with saliva. The first time he opened it he let out a huge, rumbling belch like a ship's foghorn. His ministers all clapped their hands with delight, just as if the Grand Oompah had said something very wise and important.

The four prisoners were thrown at his feet like bits of litter, and the Purple Police stood over them sniggering and poking at them with their swords. Belinda could not contain her rage. She leapt to her feet, marched up to the nearest guard, twirled round gracefully upon one foot and, 'Ha-akkk!'. Belinda's flying kick gave the poor guard such a blow that he shot backwards and knocked over seven others before finally hitting the floor himself.

'Temper, temper!' bubbled the Grand Oompah, peering down at the struggling heap. 'My goodness, what a way for a young lady to behave. Allow me to introduce myself. I am the Grand Oompah of Pomposity, Mighty Lord of the Turnback Mountains, Great Grandee of the Forest of Shadows, Commander-in-Chief of Everything-I-Look-At and what's more, I own the sky.'

'Don't be stupid,' said Belinda. 'Nobody owns the sky.'

'OH YES I DO!' roared the Grand Oompah, struggling to his feet. 'Nobody – I repeat – NOBODY dares contradict ME!'

'Temper, temper,' murmured Belinda under her breath.

The Grand Oompah collapsed back upon his throne, his face crumpling into pained lines. He gingerly rubbed his pudgy hands along the tops of his swollen, bandaged legs. He was suffering very badly from gout, for the truth of the matter was that although the Grand Oompah looked like a fish, he ate like a pig. The Royal Doctor had warned him that he would get gout as a result and now he had and his feet were exceedingly painful. The doctor had put the ruler on a diet of cabbage, and nothing else.

'Well,' burbled the Grand Oompah. 'Let's see who we have here. Mulligatawny! My dear – what an unexpected surprise. I thought you had escaped.

But you've come back.' The Oompah leaned forward and his eyes narrowed to dangerous slits. 'Tell me, why have you come back?'

'I forgot my toothbrush,' growled Mulligatawny. The Grand Oompah threw back his enormous head and laughed momentarily. Then an ugly scowl spread across his face.

'Don't lie to me, you scrawny old bag of bones, or I'll have you boiled with my cabbage for supper.'

'You're mad,' Belinda interrupted.

The Oompah leapt to his feet, his face purple with rage. 'Nobody dares speak to the Grand Oompah like that! Guards – boil these preposterous prisoners at once, and don't even bother with any salt or pepper.'

Scragg and Fink bravely froze on the spot. That left Mulligatawny and Belinda facing over thirty well-armed Purple Police. If only Knackerleevee had been with them! There was no way they could escape and they were quickly seized. Belinda desperately tried to think of a plan.

'I can stop your gout!' she cried. 'I can take away all the pain!'

'Liar!' screeched the Oompah. 'Nobody can. It's incurable.'

'How do you know until you've tried?' Belinda yelled back. 'If it doesn't work you can still boil me with the cabbages.'

The Oompah was silent for a few moments. This was very true. He *could* still boil her if he wanted. 'Bring them back here,' he ordered, and once again the four prisoners were thrown down at his fat feet. The Oompah looked at Belinda and waved his feet at her. 'Go on then,' he sneered. 'Or be boiled.'

The Karate Princess reached inside her tunic and pulled out her wallet of acupuncture needles. The Oompah watched suspiciously as Belinda approached and pulled forward a little stool. 'Rest your foot on that, O Great Pomposity,' she said soothingly, and she helped the Grand Oompah raise his exquisitely painful foot on to the stool.

Belinda knelt down and opened out the wallet. Very slowly and very carefully she drew out the longest, sharpest needle she could find. The Oompah's eyes grew bigger and bigger and his face became whiter and whiter. The little bubbles round his mouth shrivelled and dried. 'What are you going to do?' he whispered hoarsely.

Belinda grasped the needle like a dagger and held it over the Oompah's left foot. 'Tell your guards to line up by that wall,' she said quietly, 'or I shall plunge this extremely sharp needle into your big toe, and it will be so painful that you will scream and scream and scream – unless you faint first of course.'

The Grand Oompah gulped noisily and he hastily waved at the guards until they were all neatly lined up down one side of the great hall. Mulligatawny, Fink and Scragg carefully edged their way down to the main door, while Belinda kept the needle poised over the Oompah's big left toe. From the wall the Purple Police growled and snarled and rattled their daggers and swords. The Oompah broke out into a heavy sweat.

As soon as her friends were safely through the door Belinda leapt up and raced down the long hall. The Grand Oompah struggled on to his painful feet and roared. 'After her! Boil that girl at once!'

Four of the guards were brave and stupid enough to reach the door before Belinda. She went straight for them, both arms whirling. Ker-thudd! Ha-akkk! Splip-splap-klunk! The unlucky guards suddenly discovered that they were in an unconscious heap by the side of the door.

Belinda, Mulligatawny and Scragg and Fink ran as fast as they could down the twisting corridors of the Oompah's pink castle, with what was left of the Purple Police clattering angrily after them.

4

The Last Griffin

'This way!' panted Mulligatawny, leading them down ever-narrower corridors. At last she pushed past a tiny, ancient door and they were outside. 'Come on!' the old woman encouraged. 'Almost there!'

'Almost where?' Belinda had time to say before she gave an alarmed squeak.

'Aaargh!' Suddenly she found herself falling headlong, arms and legs whirling and then THUNK! She hit the ground. 'Ow!' she cried, and then 'Ow! Ouch!' as first Scragg and then Fink fell on top of her.

Mulligatawny was already on her feet, rapidly running a thick rope through her gnarled hands. Belinda struggled up from the bottom of the pile. They were on a wooden platform, which the old lady was lowering as fast as she could down into a gaping black cave. The dripping rock walls closed in round the makeshift lift, and the eerie blackness gradually swallowed them whole.

Above them the Purple Police stood on the edge of the mine-shaft and hurled abuse at the escapees. 'You can't escape! We'll be after you with the Mighty Mole!'

'Mighty Mole?' asked Belinda, wondering if the Grand Oompah had some gigantic tame mole he could unleash upon them.

'The digging machine,' explained Scragg. 'It's called the Mighty Mole. It's terrifying. It makes this dreadful noise – skrerrrr-unkk-unkk. . .'

'No,' said Fink. 'It's not like that at all. It goes skrrunng-skrrunnger-nud-nud-nud.'

'Skkunng-ker-nud-nud-nud! You must be deaf,' snarled Scragg.

'You ARE deaf,' Fink hissed, but before the quarrel could worsen, the wooden platform lurched to a halt at the bottom of the shaft.

It was dark, very dark. Belinda's heart was thumping away and Scragg and Fink instinctively held hands. Mulligatawny gave a low whistle. There was a pause and then an answering whistle, from some way off. Mulligatawny whistled again and then they saw a distant light, which began to move towards them.

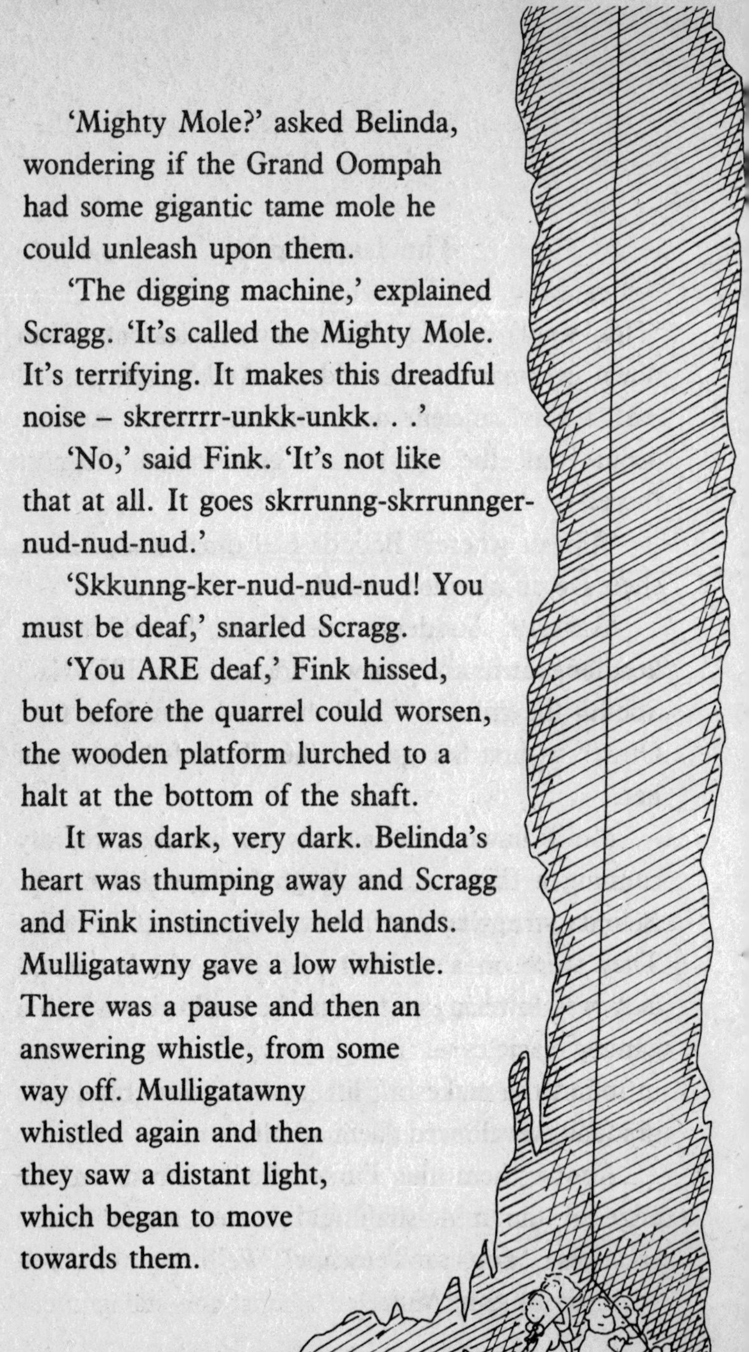

After several minutes Belinda realised that the light was in fact a flaming torch and eventually a thin, bony, grey-haired man approached, holding the torch in front of him until he recognised Mulligatawny. His dirt-streaked face cracked into a delighted grin. 'You made it then, you sly old walnut.' He sized up Belinda with one quick look. 'Is this the one who's supposed to save us? The Karate Princess? She doesn't look strong enough to lift a few pebbles.'

Mulligatawny put a hand on Belinda's shoulder. 'Let me introduce you to Blister, leader of the slave-people. The slave-people live in these caves, where they are forced to mine out the pink stone for the Grand Oompah. I'm afraid he doesn't think much of you – you know what men are like – all pride and self-esteem.'

Belinda stifled a snort of laughter. Personally, she thought this was a bit rich coming from Mulligatawny, who was for ever boasting about her own talents. Nevertheless, it was clear from the scowl on Blister's face that the Karate Princess would have to prove herself yet again.

Belinda selected a rather nice stalagmite, as thick as a big tree trunk. She walked round it once, steadied her breathing, concentrated her thoughts and then launched herself at the massive lump of rock. 'Haaaaa-aaaa-shunkkkkk!'

Her bare hand thudded against the stalagmite.

It shuddered, rocked and all at once shattered into a thousand slivers of rock which exploded across the dark floor of the cave. Belinda rubbed a speck of dirt from her hand and smiled at the astonished Blister.

'She can do acupuncture as well,' observed Mulligatawny dryly.

Blister drew back several paces, wondering what kind of self-defence acupuncture was. 'She'll do,' he croaked suspiciously.

'How many of you are there down here?' asked Belinda.

'About four hundred and fifty. Been here for years. There's no way out – there are Purple Police everywhere. We have to dig out the pink stone for the Oompah. He sends down food, mostly cabbage. We haven't seen our families for years. Most of us are pretty weak and feeble.' Blister sat down on the remaining stump of the stalagmite and gave a snort. 'What hope is there? I'd like to see *you* get us out.'

Belinda glanced at Mulligatawny. 'The guards are the biggest difficulty,' said Belinda. 'They are very well armed and dangerous. Suppose we could get hold of the Mighty Mole?'

'The digging machine?' Blister shook his head slowly. 'You'd have to be mad to try and get that.'

'What would you do with it? asked Mulligatawny.

'We could dig a way out of the mines for a start. We could even dig a way out through the Turnback Mountains.'

This idea was so staggering that everybody was silent. At last the old inventor cackled. 'You've got a good imagination, Princess.'

'Can you think of anything better?' demanded Belinda, annoyed at the unenthusiastic response to her idea.

'Can't think of anything better,' grumbled Blister. 'But I can think of lots of things that are *safer*.'

'I bet you can,' retorted Belinda quickly. 'But if you really want to get out of here then the digging machine is probably our best and only chance. However, before we do anything about that we have to find the Last Griffin.'

'Doesn't exist,' muttered Blister, picking at a large scab on his knee.

Belinda took a deep breath. She was beginning to think that deep underground was the best place for Blister and that maybe he ought to stay there for ever. 'You aren't much help, are you?' she snapped.

'Well, nobody's seen him, or her, or it, or whatever it is,' Blister said.

'We are going to search for him,' insisted Belinda. 'I want you to take us to the deepest mine shaft there is. We'll start there.'

'Waste of time,' said Blister, but he got wearily to his feet and plodded off down a dark cleft in the rock.

The rescue party followed behind but it was hard going. Sometimes they had to squeeze through narrow openings. And there were times when they had to wade waist-deep through freezing, murky water. They banged their heads. They grazed their elbows and bruised their legs a thousand times.

After an hour or so of stumbling and cursing Blister eventually called a halt. He turned to Belinda. 'This is the deepest mine. It goes no further.' He waved his torch round the shaft. 'As you can see the place is full of griffins.'

Belinda ignored him. 'Hold that torch higher,' she told him, and she began to wander round the small chamber, feeling the walls with her fingers. Blister smirked.

'Going to karate chop through solid rock now, are you?'

Belinda sighed. She'd had quite enough of this. She faced Blister with a disarming smile. 'Tell me,' she began cheerfully. 'What has two legs but can't run, can't walk, and can't stand up?'

Blister screwed up his weasel-face and at last shook his head. 'Don't know.'

'You,' said Belinda, and she gave the slave-leader a light karate chop that left him lying senseless on the cold floor. Belinda caught the flaming torch as it tumbled from his hand. She glanced at Mulligatawny. 'Now perhaps we can get on without having to listen to that idiot. Come over here. I think I may have found a crack we can get through.'

Sure enough there was a very thin split in the rock-face. Belinda just managed to squeeze her slim body into the crack, but Mulligatawny found it impossible to follow. Scragg and Fink had no luck either.

'I'll go on,' she shouted back to them. 'I'll need the torch with me.'

'Take care,' the old woman called.

'Don't be scared,' cried Fink, his teeth chattering with fear.

'Be brave like us,' squeaked Scragg, furiously chewing his nails. 'It's dark in here,' he muttered. 'Dark as Death.'

'Dark as darkest night,' whimpered Fink.

'Dark as pitch black when you can't see anything at all,' Scragg trembled.

'Dark as darkest darkness,' Fink whispered, 'when big creepy things that you can't see come creep-creeping right up to you and grab you and go BOO!'

'Aaaargh!' screamed Scragg. 'Something's grabbed me.'

'Something's grabbed ME!' yelled Fink. 'Heeelpp!'

'For heaven's sake,' shouted Mulligatawny. 'You've grabbed each other!'

Belinda giggled quietly to herself and pressed on. Holding the torch above her head, she edged carefully, one foot at a time, along the gap. At last the crack began to open out. Belinda breathed more freely and stepped out into a new, unexplored cavern. She raised the torch higher and gazed around.

The cavern was huge, with a ceiling as high as a cathedral. Long, elegant stalactites hung down, glistening with fresh water that dripped endlessly from their crystal points. Stalagmites, thick and knobbly, rose from the floor to meet them. Everywhere the rock walls glittered and shone with tiny pin-points of gold.

The Karate Princess stepped into the centre of the great cavern, her eyes wide with wonder. And then she froze, for right in front of her, almost at her very feet, she saw a large, huddled shape.

Belinda stared. She was just able to make out a big body. It appeared to have wings folded against its sides, and four legs. Yet the sleeping head was like that of a great eagle. She could clearly see its huge, powerful beak. It could only be the Last Griffin.

At that moment the Griffin woke with a start. His wings flapped angrily, causing a great rush of air that almost bowled Belinda over. The creature rose to his feet and pawed the ground with razor-sharp claws. Then he glared straight at Belinda with burning eagle-eyes.

5

Problems

The Griffin stretched his neck and cleared his throat, giving a long, low gargling kind of noise before finally speaking. 'One thousand nine hundred and seventy two,' he said mournfully. Belinda frowned.

'One thousand, nine hundred and seventy two what?' she asked.

'Years, my dear. Years. That is how long I have been waiting here for someone to find me.'

'Oh,' murmured Belinda, not being quite sure what to say next.

'Not that I've been BORED,' the Griffin added heavily. 'Far from it. Plenty to do.' He pointed his left wing around the cavern. 'Looked at that wall for almost six hundred years,' he said. 'Fascinating – absolutely fascinating. And then that wall there – four hundred and fifty years I stared at that one. Not *quite* so interesting.' He turned back to Belinda. 'And now you're here.'

'Yes.'

'Belinda – the Karate Princess.'

'You know my name!'

'But of course. I know everything. Large brain you see. Educated. Ask me a question.'

'A question? Oh – um – what was I doing before I came here?'

The Griffin threw back his head and pondered. 'Do you mean when you left Mulligatawny and those two idiotic bodyguards behind, or when you were being chased by the Purple Police, or when you were crossing the Turnback Mountains in that rickety ballooon, or when you were going to marry Hubert, or when you had a silly temper-tantrum and smashed your chest-of- '

'Stop!' laughed Belinda. 'You must be very, very clever.'

'My dear, clever does not even come into it. I am, to put it simply, stunningly brainy – not that anyone appreciates it of course. Take the Grand Oompah for example. He wants to capture me, but does he want me for my brain? Oh no.'

The Griffin settled back down on the cave floor and elegantly crossed his two front legs. 'My problem is, that being a Griffin, I have powerful magic and if someone captures me, the magic can be used by them. The Grand Oompah wants to rule the world. Absolutely no imagination that man. That's the trouble with rulers – they all get power-crazy and want to rule everything – not to mention wanting all the gold here.' The Griffin yawned in a very bored manner. 'I suppose that's why you're here too. Another bitter disappointment for me.'

'Not at all,' said Belinda. 'I've come to try and save you from the Grand Oompah.'

'Really? You and whose army?'

'Well, there's Mulligatawny and Scragg and Fink and Blister and all the slave-people . . .'

'Oh, the Oompah *will* be frightened!' The Griffin rolled his eyes and heaved an enormous sigh. 'My dear Princess, that man has more soldiers than Scragg and Fink's goose-pimples put together. He has the most highly trained and dangerous army in the world. How on earth do you propose to fight them?'

Belinda sat down cross-legged beside the Griffin and smiled up at his big, noble head. 'Actually Griffin, you are not quite as clever as I thought. I have no intention of fighting the Oompah's army.'

'No? This *is* intriguing. What *are* you going to do then?'

'I'm not absolutely sure yet. I have one or two ideas, but I do need your help.'

'How wonderful! I'm not useless after all. Silly old me, thinking I was past it.'

'We need to find a way out of here that the Purple Police don't know about,' said Belinda. 'We also need to hide you so that the Grand Oompah can't find you.'

The Griffin shook his head. 'Impossible. I have to stay here with the gold. If the Oompah finds me here then there is nothing I can do about it. If he brings the golden necklace I shall be in his power.'

'He does have the necklace,' murmured Belinda. 'Perhaps I can steal it.'

'Maybe you can, but I shall still have to stay here.' The Griffin paused and glanced around the chamber. 'In this glorious, exciting, scintillating . . . cave.' He made the last word sound like a prison door slamming upon him forever.

'There do seem to be a lot of problems,' Belinda sighed. 'There's only one thing for it. We shall just have to steal the Mighty Mole.'

'More easily said than done. It's guarded night and day. Even Mulligatawny is no longer allowed near it,' said the Griffin.

'You're not very encouraging, are you?' complained Belinda.

'My dear, for almost two thousand years I have sat here and thought – someone will come soon. Someone to talk to. Someone to play "I SPY" with. Someone to swop recipes with. But nobody came. I used to play Hide and Seek with myself you know. I'd close my eyes, count to ten, open them and shout, "Aha! I've found me!". Encouraging? What have I got to be encouraging about?'

The Griffin did indeed appear very glum and despite his complaints Belinda felt sorry for him. She got to her feet and put one arm round his massive shoulders. 'We'll find someone for you,' she said. 'A friend.' The Griffin shook his head.

'No use. I'm the last one. The Last Griffin.'

The Karate Princess stood there a few moments hugging him, wishing that there was something else [illegible] could [illegible] cheer him up, but she knew he was right. Ev[illegible] there were other things that needed seeing to. [illegible] had to get back to the others and tell them she had found the Griffin. At least they now knew where he was and so they had a slim chance of stopping the Oompah getting to him. But she still had to rescue the slave-people, *and* get hold of the Mighty Mole so that they could dig their way out of trouble.

'I must go,' she said quietly. 'But I shall be back. Wish me luck.'

But the Last Griffin had sunk into a mournful daydream and did not hear. Belinda left the cave and returned to the end of the mine-shaft. She found the others helping a rather groggy Blister to his wobbly feet. They crowded round eagerly and Belinda told them her news as quickly as she could. Even Blister hung upon her every word, and when she announced that the next task was to capture the Mighty Mole he became positively excited.

'I know a path that will take us close to the machine,' he said.

'How many guards are there?' Belinda asked.

'Forty.'

'Forty!' That was a lot. Belinda couldn't cope with forty guards by herself. Perhaps they could pick them off one by one? She sat down on a rock and tried to work out what to do. Hubert, her home and her friends seemed so very far away. She missed Hubert dreadfully, and Knackerleevee too. The Karate Princess was beginning to wonder if she would ever see them again.

Meanwhile, far above the mines, the Grand Oompah of Pomposity was not wasting time. He had been very busy. First of all he had a major temper-tantrum because Belinda and her companions had escaped. He had only calmed down after boiling three Purple Policemen with his lunch-time cabbages.

After this the Oompah had a good think about what to do next. He desperately wanted to know why Mulligatawny had returned. The old bag had managed to escape and yet she had deliberately come back, bringing that odd girl Belinda with her. There was something very fishy going on. Those rebels wouldn't have dared come back for something small and insignificant, such as a toothbrush – not that the Oompah had ever believed Mulligatawny about *that*.

No – there was something important going on and he was certain that it had a lot to do with the golden necklace, and his Big Plan. They must know he was hunting the Griffin.

The Grand Oompah snapped his fingers and at once he was lifted on to his throne by a gang of twenty panting slaves. They staggered beneath the Grandee's mighty weight as they carried him across the room to an enormous chest, bound with thick metal chains and encrusted with padlocks. One by one the Oompah undid the many locks until at last the lid of the chest flew open.

He leaned down from his throne, reached inside and pulled out a long, thin gold necklace that sparkled through his fingers like a golden waterfall. The Oompah smiled. It seemed such a small piece of jewellery and yet it held such power! No matter if Mulligatawny and the wretched girl *did* find the Griffin. They did not have the necklace; but he, The Grand, The Great, The Glorious Oompah of Pomposity *did* have it, and he intended to use it.

It was time to send out the Mighty Mole to track down the Griffin. That incredible machine could burrow through rock as if it were butter. Suddenly the Oompah clutched the necklace and gave a strangled cry. Hah! Of course! Why hadn't he realised it sooner? That was why Mulligatawny and her friends had returned. She was planning to steal back her digging machine so that they could find the Griffin!

The Oompah rubbed his chubby hands together. A deliciously wonderful idea had just occurred to him. He would leave the Mighty Mole lying around, with maybe just a sprinkling of Purple Police to make it look as though it was still being guarded. The rebels would certainly try and steal it and that would save the Oompah a lot of trouble, because then the rest of his army could rush out and capture them all in one swoop. What a lot of boiling there would be! The Oompah delicately replaced the necklace and locked the chest.

A cluster of happy bubbles popped up around the Oompah's open mouth and he gave a little giggle. What fun it was to be so clever, and so powerful! Very soon, with the help of the Griffin's magic, he would be able to send out his army and conquer the world. Then every single living creature would be his slave and he would make them build him pink castles everywhere, and eat cabbage for the rest of their lives.

6

Disaster Strikes

Several pairs of eyes peered carefully from around a clutter of boulders and scrubby plants. A short dash from their hiding place lay the Mighty Mole. Belinda had to admit that she was impressed by the massive machine. Mulligatawny had once built a steam-dragon that was pretty large, but it was dwarfed by this monster.

Like the steam-dragon it was made largely from metal plates bolted together. The front end dipped towards a sharp, wide snout and Belinda could see that the snout contained a series of tooth-edged scoops that scrabbled at the rock, one after the other, as the machine moved forward. To make it move the Mighty Mole had four curious legs. They were a little bit like wheels, except that where there would usually have been spokes, Mulligatawny had put strong, clawed legs that flailed round, gripping the ground and shoving the monster forwards.

'It's incredible,' Belinda whispered. 'What makes it work?'

'Hmmmm, it *is* quite clever, isn't it?' replied the old inventor with a great deal of pride. 'Steam. That's what makes it go – like the dragon. There's a very large boiler inside that has to be fed with wood. The steam drives the feet round.' Mulligatawny cast her eyes beyond the digging-machine. 'I can only see ten guards,' she said suspiciously.

'Biff-baff-boff!' hissed Scragg. 'We'll get 'em!'

'Yeah, we'll wring their necks,' muttered Fink.

'Pull their legs off,' added Scragg. 'And their arms.'

'Yeah – biff-boff-baff!'

'I told you!' shouted Scragg, turning on his friend. 'It's biff-baff-boff, not biff-boff-baff, half-brain.'

'No-brain!' retorted Fink, and they threw themselves at each other. Belinda quickly separated them, fixing both with a stern glare.

'Shut-up you two,' she snapped. 'There may be more guards hidden away. The best plan would be for me to tackle this little group by myself . . .'

'You can't fight ten at once!' Blister cried.

Mulligatawny gave a sly cackle and nudged the Karate Princess. The old lady had seen what Belinda could do more than once. 'I shall sort out this lot,' Belinda went on. 'If any more guards appear then you'll have to come out and do the best you can.'

Quietly she got to her feet and approached the Mighty Mole.

'Halt!' shouted one of the Purple Police, and the other nine instantly turned towards the intruder, eyes glinting from behind their purple masks. 'Who are you? What do you want?' The police looked carefully all around. They were obviously expecting more than just Belinda.

'Me?' answered Belinda with an innocent smile. 'I was just looking.'

'You're not allowed to look. You're under arrest,' snapped the Purple Police and they closed in on her.

Behind her rock, Mulligatawny closed her eyes and stuck her fingers in her ears. She knew what was going to happen and couldn't bear to watch. The others hadn't seen the Karate Princess in action before, and so they witnessed the whole sorry mess.

Swords flashed in the sunlight. The Purple Police yelled fiercely and threw themselves upon the Princess, only to immediately find themselves flying backwards at very high speed, feeling as if they had just been hit by a supersonic steam-roller.

'Urrrgh!' One of them hit a rock wall and slid down unconscious.

'Ow!' Another twirled gracefully through the air before landing face-down in the dirt.

'Eeeek!' A third came skidding out of the battle, bouncing several times on his backside before getting to his feet and running for cover. The cries died away, the dust settled and revealed the remaining seven guards neatly tied up in a big lump with their own purple scarves. Belinda wiped the dirt from her hands.

'How did she *do* that?' chorused Scragg and Fink.

'Sssh,' murmured Mulligatawny. 'Wait a moment and see if there are any other guards around.'

Several minutes passed and nothing happened. Everyone began to relax and they climbed out from their hiding place. Belinda was congratulated again and again, and Scragg and Fink marched round the purple prisoners snarling at them. 'We showed you – hah! Biff-baff-boff! Got the lot of you!'

'Got the lot of YOU!' a squeaky voice giggled. Belinda looked up and her heart sank. They were surrounded. Almost a hundred soldiers hemmed them in on every side and at the far end sat the Grand Oompah on his great throne.

'Oh dear,' he went on. 'Such a shame – just when you thought you had the digging-machine. Just when you thought you were about to ruin my Big Plan. Just when you thought you had saved the Last Griffin.'

The Oompah rubbed his hands together with immense satisfaction and his mouth produced such a cluster of bubbles that his entire face vanished for a few seconds. 'Well, I have got news for you, my little group of would-be rebels. Whilst you have been busily falling into my cunning trap I have captured the Griffin myself!'

The news came like a body-blow to them

all. They stared at each other in stunned, defeated silence. It did not go unnoticed by the Oompah, who was tickled pink to see their surprise and discomfort. 'Yes, I'm afraid so, my five little cabbages. Not only have I caught you, but I have captured the Griffin too. Now nothing – NOTHING – can stop me from becoming the first man to rule the entire world. Ho-hum, life is such *fun*, don't you think! Guards – take them to the pink castle at once, there is no time to be lost – I have the whole world to conquer!'

There was nothing to be done except follow the guards in the direction of the Oompah's castle. 'I can't believe we fell for such a simple trap,' muttered Mulligatawny. The Karate Princess dragged her feet.

'We didn't,' she said, so quietly that Mulligatawny thought she must have misheard the Princess.

'What?'

'We didn't. I want to get inside the pink castle. Allowing ourselves to be captured is the quickest way to do that.'

'But what. . . ?' began the old woman.

'Ssssh,' advised Belinda. 'Just try and look defeated.'

The Grand Oompah ordered the prisoners to be taken to his Great Hall. He wanted to keep an eye on them and watch them squirming while he invaded their lands and made slaves of their people. Sure enough, there in an iron cage was the Griffin, looking so very miserable that Belinda's heart went out to him at once. As they drew closer Belinda studied the Griffin carefully. There was something strange about him that she couldn't quite put her finger on.

The prisoners were pushed roughly up against the wall. Scragg and Fink were both moaning and chewing their nails and muttering about cabbages. Blister wouldn't even speak to Belinda. He blamed her for everything. A line of Purple Police clattered up and stood to attention with their backs to the prisoners. Belinda sighed. Their situation was getting more difficult by the second.

The Oompah's throne came staggering in and the Grandee eyed his prisoners with immense satisfaction. 'I'm going to bed,' he announced. 'Time for sleepy-byes. You lot can stand there all night and when I wake up you can watch me place the golden necklace on the Last Griffin and you can kiss goodbye to freedom. Night-night, sweet dreams!'

The prisoners watched the throne disappear. All went quiet. Mulligatawny looked at the solid wall of Purple Police. 'Well Princess, you got us in here all right. How are you going to get us out?'

Belinda carefully slipped one hand inside her top and pulled out the little leather wallet. The old lady gave a low cackle. 'What are you going to do – stab them to death with a needle?'

Belinda smiled back and crept silently behind one of the guards. Holding the needle between her thumb and one finger she carefully stuck it into the Purple Policeman's bottom. The others held their breath and waited for him to leap sky-high, but the guard didn't appear to feel a thing. Belinda gave a little smile and began to twiddle the needle round and round. After a few seconds the guard's eyes

fluttered shut and he rocked gently on his feet.

Belinda moved on to a second guard, slid the needle carefully into his fat backside and repeated the process. She continued down the long line, until all the guards were quietly standing unconscious on their feet.

'There,' she said, as the last guard began to rock on his feet. 'The Oompah said it was time for bed.'

'How did you do that?' demanded an astonished Blister.

'Acupuncture,' Belinda told him. 'I would have let you all have a go but it's not something you can do without special training. It took me months to learn. Now, we've got to get out of here, but first we must release the Griffin and rescue the necklace from the Oompah's chest.

Belinda ran across to the great chest but one look at all the padlocks told her that it was going to take a bit of breaking open and the noise would certainly wake the guards. It was best to get the Griffin out first. Quickly, she slid back the bolts on the Griffin's cage.

'Take the Griffin and head for the Mighty Mole,' whispered Belinda, 'and get it started up – it's our only chance of escape. I'll follow in a few minutes. I want to get that necklace from the chest before we leave.'

'You're crazy!' Blister hissed at her. The Karate Princess gave him a big grin and nodded.

'You noticed then!' she laughed quietly. 'Now, hurry up and go! I'll catch you up.'

'Be careful,' murmured Mulligatawny, then she tiptoed out with the Griffin and the others at her heels.

Belinda passed the time by testing the collection of chains and padlocks on the massive chest. At last she decided that Mulligatawny and the others must have reached the safety of the Mighty Mole. She took several paces away from the chest, then stopped.

The Karate Princess focused her eyes in pure concentration. They almost burned into the heavy padlocks. She took a deep breath and ran straight at the chest. Just before she reached it she leapt high into the air and, with both feet flying out in front of her like a ten-ton demolition ball, she crashed on to the chest. HAAA-KRUNNNK!

Chains burst their links. Padlocks went spinning uselessly through the air. The sides of the chest split apart and the contents spilled across the palace floor. As the Purple Police snapped awake with cries of anger and alarm, Belinda snatched up the golden necklace and ran out of the Great Hall, down the long corridors and outside towards the waiting machine.

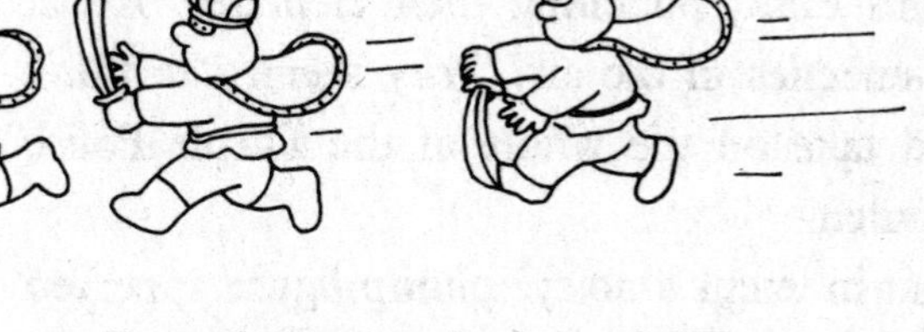

But where was the steam? Where was the heavy throb of the pulsing engine? A small hatch at the front of the Mole was flung open and Mulligatawny stuck out her head. 'It won't start!' she yelled to the Princess. 'The stupid thing won't start! The Purple Police are coming! We're all going to be caught – do something, Belinda!
DO SOMETHING!!'

7

The Great Escape

Belinda skidded to a halt and gazed frantically all around. Purple Police were beginning to appear from the castle. The full moonlight flashed on their drawn weapons.

'Fight them Belinda! Biff-baff-boff!' chorused Scragg and Fink, punching their clenched fists at invisible enemies in the air. They seemed to think she could take on the whole of the Purple Police single-handed.

At that moment a noisy, plump figure appeared on the balcony. The Grand Oompah of Pomposity gripped the railings with white knuckles and roared furiously at his guards. 'Grab her, you big fat baboons! Get the water boiling! I want some cabbages! Get her!' And he delivered an enormous belch like the roar of a cannon.

Belinda's gaze went from the Oompah to the balcony, and from the balcony to the complicated framework of wooden scaffolding that still clung to the Oompah's pink castle. Meanwhile the Purple Police hesitated. None of them wished to be the first to tackle the Karate Princess. Many of them were already sporting bandages because of their previous encounters with her. Their hesitation gave Belinda just the breathing space she needed, and she set off at full speed, racing straight for the Purple Police and the castle.

The guards clustered together and rattled their weapons. Belinda blasted them with the most frightening yell she could manage. 'Raaaaaaaaargh!!' The soldiers fell back from her and she burst through their weak line, hurtling towards the castle itself. She reached the bottom of the great wall and stared up at the massive scaffolding.

The Karate Princess balanced herself carefully, eyes fixed on one wooden pillar. 'No!' screamed the Oompah, suddenly realising what she had in mind, but it was too late. Belinda twisted gracefully on one foot and then her other leg shot out like a whip-crack and crunched against the scaffolding. KERRRUNNKKKK!!!!

The pole split. It cracked. It bent. It snapped and as it did so a whole series of wooden pillars began to collapse, one after the other. The scaffolding began to tumble from the castle walls in a roar of wood upon wood. Belinda dashed for the digging machine. Behind her, pink rocks started to crash down from the battlements. They smashed amongst the broken poles and clouds of dust rose up, smothering everything until only the noise of the collapsing castle could be heard – an endless, grinding, thunderous ruination.

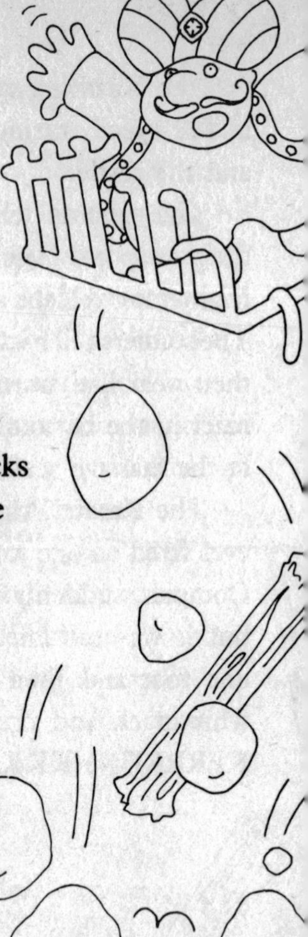

The Karate Princess jumped into the Mighty Mole, which was at last hissing steam from every crack and Blister slammed the door shut behind her. A grinding jerk threw them all to the floor, but it was only the machine getting under way as Mulligatawny took the controls. The tooth-edged scoops began to clatter round and the Mighty Mole dug down into the rocky earth. The escapees grinned happily at each other as the machine left its pursuers far behind.

'We showed them!' cried Fink. 'Boff-biff-baff!'

'Yeah,' agreed Scragg, who by this time was so muddled he couldn't remember if it was biff-baff-boff, biff-boff-baff, baff-biff-boff or what.

'Where do you want me to go?' asked Mulligatawny.

'Can you find your way down to the Last Griffin?' Belinda asked.

'Of course, but why go there? We've got him on board already.'

'I don't think so,' smiled the Princess, and she turned to the Griffin. 'You're safe with us now,' she explained to the trembling creature. 'But where did the Grand Oompah find you?'

The Griffin's dark eyes were wet with tears. 'I was searching by a river in the Turnback Mountains. I was high up, well above the snow-line. I thought I would be safe there and I had to carry on the search.'

'Search for what?' the old lady shouted back over one shoulder, as she piloted the machine deep underground.

'The golden necklace,' the Griffin sighed. 'It was lost almost two thousand years ago and I have been hunting it ever since, for I am the Last Griffin and I must find it.'

'Your search is over,' said Belinda, drawing the delicate chain from her pocket. 'I have the golden necklace right here.' The Griffin gave a gasp and then bowed her head sadly.

'Then I have lost after all, and you have power over me forever.'

'But I don't want power over you,' laughed Belinda. 'Here, the chain is yours,' and she laid it gently at the Griffin's feet. 'What's more, I have to tell you that you are NOT the Last Griffin.'

Before Belinda could explain, the Mighty Mole ground to a halt and Mulligatawny declared that they had arrived at the Last Griffin's cavern. 'Mind you, I have to say that I am most confused,' muttered the old inventor. 'Hmmm, all this talk about more than one griffin – what *is* going on?'

The Karate Princess opened the machine's door and they all stepped into the Griffin's gold-specked cave. 'Allow me to introduce you all to the Last Griffin,' Belinda cried, pointing to the Griffin as it came wearily towards them. 'Last Griffin, please let me introduce the other Last Griffin.'

A long, stunned silence followed. Belinda was right. There were two Griffins, and they stood and stared, and stared and stood and stared again. Eventually the First Griffin (since he can no longer be called the Last Griffin) gave out a deep sigh.

'I see. I have spent almost two thousand years down here quite unnecessarily? All those games I played by myself I could have played *with* someone?' He glared at the Second Griffin. 'The object of playing Hide and Seek,' he said very heavily indeed, 'is NOT to hide for two thousand years, but to let yourself be found so that the other person can JOIN IN.'

'I didn't know you existed,' said the Second Griffin. 'I thought I was the last. I'm so pleased that you are here. You're very handsome,' she added, and fluttered her eyelashes. For once the First Griffin was too stunned to speak.

Something about this conversation made Belinda's heart lurch. All at once she remembered that she had a partner at home. Hubert and Knackerleevee and her parents must be worried to death wondering what had happened to her. It was time to finish off her work.

'We must hurry,' she said. 'Everyone back into the machine. Blister, it is time to say goodbye. You must go and find your people and bring them back here. The Mighty Mole will carry on tunnelling right beneath the Turnback Mountains. All you have to do is follow the tunnel and eventually you and your people will be free. Good luck!'

Blister gave her a delighted grin, flung himself at the Princess and wrapped her in an enormous hug. A moment later he vanished into the darkness to find the slave-people.

Several hours later the rock-caked snout of the Mighty Mole broke through to the other side of the mountains and came to a halt. The engines that had worked so hard slowly subsided into an almost silent hissing. Scragg pushed back the door and sunlight flooded into the belly of the machine. 'We've done it,' murmured Mulligatawny, with deep satisfaction, gazing up at the great mountains that now lay behind them.

The two Griffins, who were now free to roam the deserted mountains in peace, came to say their goodbyes. Spreading their great wings they launched themselves into the blue air. They circled a couple of times, diving down low over Belinda and her friends before climbing higher and heading off into the unknown snow-lined valleys of the mountains.

As the Griffins disappeared from view the first of the slave-people began to struggle out from the mouth of the newly-dug tunnel. They blinked at the bright sunlight, their smudged faces full of joy. They ran across the ground, turned cartwheels, leapt in the air and gave each other piggy-backs. More and more appeared – old and young, men and women and children – all laughing and shouting, until eventually a great happy chant rose from the crowd.

'Oompah! Oompah! You're a silly Oompah!
Pick a cabbage, boil a cabbage,
Stick it up your Joompah!'

And then came the remains of the Purple Police. They staggered out from the tunnel. They were without weapons and threw themselves at Belinda's feet. 'Let us escape too,' they pleaded. 'We cannot bear to work for that cabbage-maniac any longer!' And so it was that the Grand Oompah found himself with only half an army, no Griffin, no necklace, no slaves, no castle and no power. All he had left were his cabbages, his gout and his bad manners.

Belinda noted all this with great satisfaction. She knew that the Grand Oompah was no longer a threat. She turned and hugged Mulligatawny.

'What's that for?' grunted the old lady.

'I'm saying goodbye.'

'Hmmm. Typical. I take all this trouble and I *still* don't get invited to the wedding.'

Belinda turned very red. 'Oh Mulligatawny, I'm so sorry. Of course you are invited. Now, what will be quickest – going by foot or in your monster machine here?'

The old lady grinned. 'Just watch this. Now that we are above ground the Mighty Mole can really show a turn of speed!' They climbed back inside and with a great belch of steam the machine was off. For an hour or so Belinda sat next to Mulligatawny, watching the countryside vanish beneath the spinning metal legs of the machine. Then she fell into a deep, peaceful sleep.

8

The Knot is Tied

'Wake up! Rise and shine!' The Queen pulled back Belinda's curtains and sunlight splashed across the bed. Belinda stirred.

'What? What day is it?'

'Your second wedding day!' cried the Queen. 'Come on, you've been asleep ever since Mulligatawny brought you back. We've heard all about your adventures and you must have been very tired but really dear, you can't keep Hubert waiting any longer – not to mention your poor father. I think he'll explode if he doesn't see you married today. Look, I mended your wedding dress while you were swanning around in hot-air balloons and the like.'

Belinda sat up and glanced at the birthday cake draped over her mother's arm. Everything, it seemed, was back to normal.

Outside, Knackerleevee almost hugged her to death. At last he could be Bestest Man. And then there was Hubert. (To spare any blushes we shall hurry on to the wedding itself.)

Two surprise guests turned up: the Griffins. 'We had to come,' said the Second Griffin, with the golden necklace twinkling round her neck. 'You did so much for us.'

'I suppose you're having a party?' demanded the First Griffin. 'I don't mind putting in a guest-appearance,' he added, inviting himself on the spot.

That same afternoon saw everyone gathered once more on the castle lawn. Knackerleevee was bursting out of his wedding-suit. All Belinda's sisters gathered round the happy couple. Hubert looked very handsome and the Karate Princess thought she was the luckiest girl in the world. The priest stepped forward and began the ceremony.

'I do!' cried Hubert, ten minutes later.

'I do!' Belinda shouted to the sky and anyone who happened to be listening. King Stormbelly rushed up to the priest.

'They ARE married, aren't they? Please say it's legal this time. PLEASE!'

'I pronounce you man and wife,' said the priest solemnly.

This time it was King Stormbelly who fainted, whilst all around him a great cheer went up and the celebrations began. Belinda slipped quietly to one side and handed Mulligatawny a small, but sharp acupuncture needle.

'If you want to wake my father from his fainting fit, just stick this in him,' she said.

'Hmmmm – anywhere in particular, Princess?'

Belinda grinned back at the old lady. 'Oh, I think anywhere will do!' she giggled, and she hurried back to join her husband and the party.